MOUNTAIN BIKING

36
VAL DI SOLE
TRENTINO
SCHWALBE

MOUNTAIN BIKING

ODYSSEYS

JIM WHITING

CREATIVE EDUCATION · CREATIVE PAPERBACKS

Published by Creative Education and Creative Paperbacks
P.O. Box 227, Mankato, Minnesota 56002
Creative Education and Creative Paperbacks
are imprints of The Creative Company
www.thecreativecompany.us

Design by Blue Design (www.bluedes.com)
Production by Joe Kahnke
Art direction by Rita Marshall
Printed in the United States of America

Photographs by Alamy (Hemis, Andrew Lloyd, NicVW, sport, STOCK4B GmbH, Westend61 GmbH), Creative Commons Wikimedia (Photo by DAVID ILIFF. License: CC-BY-SA 3.0; Knud Bergslien), Dreamstime (Kaliszuk), Getty Images (Hyoung Chang/Denver Post, Tim Clayton/Corbis Sport, Blake Jorgenson/Aurora, Christian Petersen/Getty Images Sport, Popperfoto, Oli Scarff/Getty Images News), iStockphoto (tassapon), Marin Museum of Bicycling (Larry Cragg/Wende Cragg Galleries), Shutterstock (AMatveev, homydesign, Maciej Kopaniecki, ntdanai, PHOTOMDP), University of Montana Mansfield Library (Photo 73.0031: Frank M. Ingalls Photographs, Archives and Special Collections)

Library of Congress Cataloging-in-Publication Data
Names: Whiting, Jim, author.
Title: Mountain biking / Jim Whiting.
Series: Odysseys in extreme sports.
Includes bibliographical references and index.
Summary: An in-depth survey of the popular extreme sport of mountain biking, from its first informal downhill races to the grueling annual Birkebeiner, as well as its records and famous bikers.
Identifiers: LCCN 2017028048 / ISBN 978-1-60818-693-8 (hardcover) / ISBN 978-1-62832-289-7 (pbk) / ISBN 978-1-56660-729-2 (eBook)

Subjects: LCSH: Mountain biking—Juvenile literature.
Classification: LCC GV1056 .W47 2018 / DDC 796.63—dc23

CCSS: RI 8.1, 2, 3, 4, 5, 8, 10; RI 9-10.1, 2, 3, 4, 5, 8, 10; RI 11-12.1, 2, 3, 4, 5, 10; RST 6-8.1, 2, 5, 6, 10; RST 9-10.1, 2, 5, 6, 10; RST 11-12.1, 2, 5, 6, 10

CONTENTS

onde a natureza vive
penacova
MUNICIPIO
vodafone
405
SHIMANO
SIXPACK

Introduction

Soured on soccer? Fed up with football? Bored by baseball? Turned off by team sports? If so, extreme sports might be more to your liking. While there's not an exact definition of what makes a sport "extreme," the following characteristics (or at least most of them) seem to be common: a higher degree of risk despite use of protective gear, emphasis on achieving high speeds and/or

OPPOSITE: Mountain bike racing is offered in many forms to satisfy a wide range of interests and skill levels. Some courses are flat, while others drop down steep hills, skirt the edges of a cliff, or wind through the woods.

heights, more likely to be performed alone or with a handful of friends, no issues with playing time as in team sports, stunts requiring substantial amounts of skill and practice, less emphasis on formal rules, and an **adrenaline** rush from physical exertion.

Not long ago, many bicyclists wanted a challenge greater than riding through city streets while dodging cars, trucks, and buses. They found the answer by riding mountain bikes in the hills and forests beyond their urban environment. On dirt trails and rough fire roads in the wilderness, they covered far more territory and enjoyed the solitude of nature while becoming physically fit. Some riders prefer freeriding, going cross-country over a variety of terrain. Others like downhill. They ride to the top of a steep slope, then zoom back down at breathtaking speeds.

Mountain Biking Backstory

The first bicycle appeared in Germany in 1817. Called the *laufmaschine* (running machine), it was powered by a person sitting in the seat and using his legs and feet to propel the device. About 20 years later, primitive pedals allowed riders to move their bikes mechanically and achieve faster speeds.

Designers realized that the

OPPOSITE The high-wheeler was also known as a penny-farthing. In England, a farthing was a coin smaller than a penny. The size difference between the coins reflected the relative sizes of the wheels.

larger the front wheel, the farther and faster the bike would travel with each stroke of the pedals. That led to the ordinary, or high-wheeler, in the early 1870s. With a front wheel as large as five feet (1.5 m) across and a much smaller rear wheel, the ordinary was the first extreme bicycle. Just getting onto the seat was challenging. And once underway, riders could achieve the then unheard-of speed of 20 miles (32.2 km) per hour.

Riding ordinaries wasn't for the faint-hearted. Because riders were mounted so high and so far forward, any collision would almost certainly pitch them forward. They would hit the ground with such force that they would often break both wrists. Sometimes tumbles happened so quickly that they landed directly on their heads and occasionally even died of a fractured skull. No one wore protective headgear in that era.

Buffalo Soldiers

The first mountain bikers may have been about 20 members of the all-black 25th Infantry Regiment. Commanded by Lt. James Moss, the group tested the military value of specially modified bicycles in the Rocky Mountains area in 1896. Carrying all their supplies, they began with a 4-day, 126-mile (203 km) trek in the Rockies. Soon afterward, they covered 800 miles (1,287 km) in similar terrain in 23 days. The following year, they rode nearly 2,000 miles (3,219 km) from Missoula, Montana, to St. Louis, Missouri. En route, they encountered torrential rains, rattlesnakes, wretched roads, and a series of sand hills in Nebraska that forced them to detour and bounce along railroad ties amid 110 °F (43.3 °C) temperatures. Moss's superiors weren't sufficiently impressed. With the Spanish-American War looming, the bicycle corps went nowhere.

Within a decade, the dangers of the ordinary led to safety bicycles, with two wheels of equal size. Improvements such as pedal-driven chains as the means of propulsion and **pneumatic tires** for a smooth ride led to a boom in cycling. The newly formed League of American Wheelmen lobbied for better roads and encouraged even more people to ride. "A person without a wheel is out of the times, as it were," Montana's *Daily Missoulian* reported in the spring of 1894.

The national enthusiasm was short-lived. Soon afterward, the invention of the automobile changed Americans' riding habits. Now they could travel much farther and with less effort than on their bikes. By the 1940s, bikes were considered to be little more than children's toys. After World War II in 1945, Americans could choose between two basic types: heavy cruising bikes made primarily by Schwinn, and lighter ones (often imported) with three speeds, hand brakes, and narrow tires. These were known as "English racers."

Almost exactly a century after the invention of the ordinary, the next wave of extreme biking began—according to most versions of the story—in Marin County, California. Located on the north end of the Golden Gate Bridge, across from San Francisco, Marin County is noted for its hilly terrain, crowned by the 2,571-foot (784 m) Mount Tamalpais. A group of riders on old Schwinn "fat tire" bikes organized a series of informal races down a fire road that dropped more than 1,300 feet (396 m) in 2 miles (3.2 km). Protective gear was minimal: boots, long-sleeve jackets, knee pads, work gloves. A few wore just jeans and T-shirts. Hardly anyone bothered with anything on their heads besides baseball caps.

The speeds they attained caused the grease in the **coaster brake** hubs to melt. After a couple of runs, the hubs needed to be repacked with fresh grease. As a result, the races became known as the "Repack Downhill." Soon afterward, the term "mountain bike" began appearing to describe the bikes that were being used.

Charlie Kelly, one of the Repack organizers, emphasizes, "Marin County is not the only place where the mountain bike was invented, but it is the birthplace of

"Marin County is not the only place where the mountain bike was invented, but it is the birthplace of the *sport* of mountain biking."

the *sport* of mountain biking." Word of the racing soon filtered out. The cycling magazine *Velo News* printed a story in 1978. The following year, a San Francisco television station aired a segment. CBS picked up the story and ran with it nationally. Kelly wrote an article for the popular adventure magazine *Outside* in 1980. Mountain biking was now becoming a part of the national sports and recreation consciousness.

The bikes themselves were undergoing a transformation. The frames of the original bikes were unsuited to such fast speeds and sharp turns. They frequently broke. Some of the Repackers, such as Joe Breeze, Gary Fisher, and Tom Ritchey, began building better, more

Joe Breeze, 1977

Repack Races

The first Repack race was staged in October 1976. Riders went off at two-minute intervals, with the faster ones going toward the end. There's a good reason why Alan Bonds won the first race. All nine of his rivals crashed. "The road is littered with in-line gullies, blind and off-camber turns, and the occasional cluster of head-size rocks," explains 10-time winner Joe Breeze. The names of some terrain features provide evidence of its hazards. Hamburger Helper Rock. Danger "X." Cuisinart. In all, there were 24 Repack races. Initially they were so popular that the first nine were held in a little more than two months. Gary Fisher, later renowned as a frame designer and builder, holds the course record of 4 minutes and 22 seconds. The final race was held in 1984.

durable frames. They added hand brakes, gears, and other improvements. In 1979, Kelly, Fisher, and Ritchey formed the first mountain bike company.

At first, traditional bike manufacturers regarded mountain biking as a fad. The big guys were wrong. As more people became interested in adventure sports that allowed participants to test themselves outdoors, mountain biking took off.

Mountain bike technology made a big advance in the early 1990s when manufacturers began adding suspension systems. These systems absorb much of the shock a rider encounters on rough roads. This absorption in turn reduces the stress on riders' hands and arms and allows them to ride in much greater comfort.

The growth in mountain biking's popularity was fueled by increasing media exposure. In 1995, the ESPN television network created the Extreme (later shortened to X) Games to highlight nontraditional sports. Mountain biking has been a fixture from the beginning. Perhaps more importantly, mountain biking made its debut in the Olympic Games the following year with a cross-country race. "For a sport to go from zero to warp speed so quickly is unprecedented," said Brian Stickel, director of competition for the National Off-Road Bicycle Association (NORBA), the governing body for mountain bike racing in the United States.

The inclusion of mountain biking in the 1996 Olympics indicated the growing internationalization of the sport. Though the sport had originated in California, it quickly took hold in cycling-friendly Europe. As a result, Europeans claimed five of the six medals. Susan DeMattei's bronze was the only American medal in that first competition.

Most mountain bikers are more interested in its recreational aspects. By the start of the 21st century, mountain bikes could be found everywhere, from Wal-Mart to specialty shops. Recent sales figures indicate that mountain bikes are the largest single segment of retail bike sales. With so many people now riding mountain bikes, manufacturers are constantly improving upon and adding to existing technology in ways that no one hurtling down the side of a steep hill just 40 years ago could have envisioned.

Twenty years after the first Repack racers careened down the hills of Marin County, mountain biking became an event in the Olympic Games. In 2016, 49 men and 29 women competed for medals in cross-country mountain biking in Rio de Janeiro, Brazil.

POLSKA
POLSKA
uvex
BRASIL
2
5
DT SWISS

Biking Basics

Mountain bikes vary considerably in cost, from stock models with basic **components** to top-end models with handmade frames and top-of-the-line components. In general, mountain bikes are heavier than road bikes, with thicker tubing and often equipped with front and/or rear suspension systems to reduce the shock of riding over rough ground.

Once you know how much you want to spend, then you need to choose

OPPOSITE: Downhill courses are generally the most dangerous. To decrease their risk of injury, riders must develop strength, endurance, and mental acuity. It is common for racers to wear a full-face helmet, gloves, and kneepads or a full-body suit.

among hardtail, full suspension, or no suspension. No suspension means a fairly hard ride, as every bump and pothole transmits the shock upward. A hardtail bike has a front suspension fork, which reduces fatigue on your hands and arms and provides better steering control. It is a good selection for beginners or for all-around basic use. Full suspension means there is both front and rear suspension. The overall ride comfort is higher, though you'll usually pay more money. A variation of full suspension is a downhill bike. It's used primarily for downhill racing and extreme downhill riding. The suspension forks have more travel and the bike has a longer **wheelbase**.

Mountain bike handlebars are flat and relatively short from tip to tip. This enables riders to maintain a more upright posture and therefore exert more control. The saddle, or seat, is especially important since you'll be spending considerable amounts of time on it. You don't need to keep the bike's original seat, if it proves to be uncomfortable. Changing seats is a simple process. It's well worth spending some extra money to find one that's a good fit for you.

While you're riding, it's best to maintain a steady cadence. Cadence refers to the number of complete revolutions of the pedals in the span of a minute. A steady cadence is relatively easy on flat ground. But if you had only a

Mountain bikes come in a variety of sizes, weights, and suspension styles. Before buying one, first decide where and how often you'll use it and how much you are willing to spend.

Hurley
animal
FOX

single gear, riding uphill would be more difficult and you couldn't maintain the same cadence.

Fortunately, mountain bikes have multiple gears. You change gears by using a derailleur. This is a French word meaning "to throw off track." A derailleur moves the chain from one gear to another by applying or releasing pressure with a cable connected to a control lever on the handlebars.

A mountain bike has both front and rear derailleurs. The front derailleur controls the chainring. This is the large front ring on a bike. It is connected to the crank and pedals. Mountain bike chainrings have three **sprockets** of different sizes. The rear derailleur controls the freewheel, which is connected to the rear hub of the bike and has as many as 10 sprockets of varying sizes. The difference in size between chainring and freewheel sprockets is known

Learning to Use Derailleurs

Two levers mounted on the handlebars control derailleur shifting. Each lever displays a range of numbers to indicate the gear—for example, 1 through 3 for the chainring and 1 through 6 for the freewheel. You usually press the lever forward with your thumb to select a lower gear, and pull it back with your index finger for a higher gear. It's best to start practicing in a flat, traffic-free area. You need to keep pedaling for shifting to go as quickly and efficiently as possible. Eventually, you can move to moderate hills. Steeper hills require considerable practice, as you could run the risk of stalling out and falling. For maximum safety, downshift just before you get to the base of the hill.

as the gear ratio. You obtain the gear ratio by dividing the number of teeth of the chainring sprocket by the number of teeth of the freewheel sprocket. For example, you may be using a chainring sprocket with 44 teeth and a freewheel sprocket with 11 teeth. Forty-four divided by 11 is 4. The higher the gear ratio, the harder it is to pedal the bike. However, a higher gear ratio also means you will go farther every time you complete a revolution.

In a bike's highest gear, the chain is on the largest front sprocket and the smallest rear sprocket. This gear is most commonly used while riding downhill. The lowest gear has the opposite configuration. You'll use this one when you're climbing an especially steep hill. In between, you can have as many as 28 different choices. Naturally there will be some overlap, as the accompanying chart shows. In general, when two gears are very similar and you need

Freewheel Teeth

Chainring Teeth	11	15	19	23	27	32
22	2.0	1.5	1.2	1.0	0.8	0.7
33	3.0	2.2	1.7	1.4	1.2	1.0
44	4.0	2.9	2.3	1.9	1.6	1.4

Gear Ratio Chart

to shift, it's easier to keep the chainring where it is and change the freewheel by using the rear derailleur. That's because freewheel changes are virtually instantaneous, but the chainring may take a couple of seconds to respond.

OPPOSITE Colder temperatures and uncertain terrain make mountain biking in the snow especially challenging. Some people let some of the air out of their tires in an attempt to stay on top of the snow. Others use fat-tire bikes on tricky surfaces like snow and sand.

Clearly, you need a way of stopping your bike. For years, mountain bikes used rim brakes. When the rider squeezed the brake lever, hard rubber pads on each side of the wheel rim were compressed against it. This compression slowed the bike and brought it to a halt.

Rim brakes don't do well in mud or wet weather. It's harder for the brake pads to grip the rim because it is so slick. This problem led to the development of disc brakes in the mid-1990s. Disc brakes are becoming standard on mid- and high-end bikes. A rotor is mounted on the wheel hub, and a **hydraulic** or cable-operated pad presses against each side of the rotor to bring the bike to a halt. While they add a little more weight than rim brakes, disc brakes are more reliable and generate greater stopping power.

Once you've picked out a bike, the next step is selecting the proper gear. Nothing is more important

than a high-quality helmet. In many places, local law requires you to wear one. In addition, riding over rough ground increases the possibility of falling off your bike and hitting your head. Modern technology has made helmets lightweight, streamlined, well-ventilated, and stylish. You may not even notice you're wearing one.

Gloves give a better grip on the handlebars. Most have padding to ease the pressure on your hands. They also provide warmth in cold weather and protection if you fall. Some have the fingertips cut off to enable more precise control.

There is a variety of additional gear to consider. Long-sleeved shirts can prevent scrapes in the event of a fall. A lightweight jacket is useful in chilly weather. Padded bike shorts help you stay on the saddle longer. If you wear long pants, be sure they fit tightly around your ankles to prevent getting caught in the chain.

When you venture off-road, you need to be prepared. Water bottles attach easily to the frame and provide hydration. Small bags containing tire patches, tools, and light snacks fit under the saddle. Be sure to have plenty of illumination—reflectors, rear lights, front lights—for riding in low-light conditions. When you ride on roads with motor vehicles, lights can help you avoid collisions. If you use a mountain bike for riding around town, you don't need knobby tires. In fact, they'll wear out more quickly on pavement than on rugged trails. You'll have a faster and smoother ride by getting a set of what are known as "slick" or "semi-slick" tires. These have a smooth **tread** that will help you zip along the streets.

Mountain biking is a great way to explore nature and enjoy scenic views while getting some exercise. Packing plenty of supplies, including water, snacks, and tire-repairing materials, will help keep the experience pleasant.

First Families and Repackers

No one is more closely associated with the origins of mountain biking than Charlie Kelly. He grew up in Mill Valley, California, in the shadow of the hills that would eventually become legendary among mountain bikers. Kelly promoted and frequently rode in the Repack races. He also had an active role in developing frames more suited to the tremendous stresses that hurtling downhill generated.

In 1980, he began publishing *Fat Tire Flyer*, the country's only mountain bike publication. Kelly did virtually everything for the magazine: writing articles, taking photos, laying it out, overseeing the printing, and maintaining the subscription base. He also wrote the book *Fat Tire Flyer* (2014), an account of the early days of mountain biking.

Kelly became one of the founders of NORBA in 1983. The steadily increasing popularity of the sport required a set of rules and regulations and a means of providing insurance. NORBA also made provisions for the selection of national champions.

Because mountain biking originated in racing, most of the sport's big names are associated with going fast. For example, in 2008, Dan Atherton became England's

OPPOSITE Despite suffering a dislocated hip, torn rotator cuff, concussions, and other injuries, professional downhill and cross-country racer Gee Atherton has piled up several World Cup wins and national championships.

national champion in downhill mountain bike racing. He seemed poised to take his skills to the next level and compete for world titles. But two years later, he broke his neck and nearly died. He said he was through with racing. But he enjoyed the sport too much. So he returned in 2012 and won several prestigious races. Yet Dan probably isn't even the best rider in his family.

His younger brother Gee (George) Atherton burst onto the world racing scene at the age of 15 and won his first International Cyclist Union (UCI) World Cup Downhill title 4 years later. A rider whose philosophy is "If you're in control, you're not going fast enough," Gee went on to become a four-time national champion, two-time world champion, and in 2013 was ranked number 1 in the world in downhill.

And in 2005, their younger sister Rachel Ather-

Red Bull
EventScotland

ton—18 at the time—was named [London] *Times* Young Sportswoman of the Year for her accomplishments in downhill racing. Three years later, she won both the UCI World Cup Downhill and the UCI World Championship. Unfortunately, in 2009, she sustained serious injuries while she was training. After taking a year off to recover, she clawed her way back into the top levels of the sport and won the same two titles in 2013, 2015, and 2016. For all these accomplishments, many people regard the Athertons as the "First Family of Mountain Biking."

Rebecca Rusch never had to worry about her siblings in making a name for herself in the sport. She had to overcome other challenges, though. Her athletic career began in high school in the early 1980s when she ran cross-country and track. A key turning point in Rusch's life came when she quit during a race because she felt sick. It left a lasting impression. "The pain of quitting far outlasts the pain of pushing forward," she wrote many years later. "By lining up for a race, I'm making a commitment—to myself, my friends, my family, my teammates, my fans—to finish, no matter what place I'm in."

As a young adult, Rusch realized that a 9-to-5 job wasn't for her. Though initially plagued by self-doubt, she began rock climbing. That led to other strenuous outdoor activities. Starting in the 1990s, she participated in the Eco-Challenge adventure race. Teams of men and women ran, biked, rode horses, and canoed for 300 miles (483 km) in remote, demanding wilderness areas around the world. The series ended in 2004 when a falling boulder killed a competitor. Rusch still had a year remaining on her sponsorship contract. The company told her to do something amazing during that year. Try mountain biking, said a friend. Rusch hated the sport. Riding had always been her weak leg in adventure racing. She entered a 100-mile (161 km) race anyway.

She had found her niche. Endurance racing national and world championship titles soon followed. And Rusch seems to get better with age. In 2013, she broke the women's record for the 138-mile (222 km) Kokopelli Trail race in Colorado and Utah by an hour and a half. She was 45 at the time. It was especially remarkable that she rode much of the time with a badly dislocated finger.

"I really am just a regular person. Physically … I'm completely average. Just ask my trainer."

Continuing despite her injury is one example of why many people refer to her as the "Queen of Pain." Rusch prefers to be known as the "Queen of Perseverance" because she never gives up. "I really am just a regular person. Physically … I'm completely average," she said. "Just ask my trainer."

When she's not on her bike competing or participating in other strenuous activities such as whitewater rafting and cross-country skiing, Rusch is a firefighter and EMT in Ketchum, Idaho. She encourages women to stretch their cycling limits through the SRAM Gold Rusch Tour. The Tour is a series of skills clinics, organized rides, and other events in various locations. Rusch is also active in charity work, serving on a number of nonprofit boards of directors.

In addition to mountain biking, Rebecca Rusch has gained fame in climbing, cross-country skiing, and whitewater rafting. Known for endurance events, she is also a motivational speaker, encouraging girls and women to take part in adventure sports.

MTB

OPPOSITE Professional cyclist Pia Sundstedt competed in Olympic road racing events in 2000 and 2012. Over that same span, Sundstedt took first place six times in the women's event of the Birkebeiner, the world's largest long-distance mountain bike race.

Like the Athertons, Pia Sundstedt of Finland illustrates the worldwide appeal of mountain biking. She is not just one of the world's best mountain bike racers, she's one of the world's top bike racers—period. She represented Finland in the 2000 and 2012 Summer Olympic Games in road cycling. Between those two appearances she took up mountain biking.

Her introduction to the sport in 2004 was less than auspicious. "It was technically difficult and there were thousands of mosquitos," she recalled. She gave the sport another shot the following year and entered the European Championships. "No one knew me, I went to a used bike, and without sponsors," she explained. "I went in a blur, I knew that no one could beat me on that day." That title was the prelude to her winning the UCI World Cup Cross-Country Marathon in 2006. She defended her title the next two years and added a fourth championship in 2011. As of 2017, she had also won six Birkebeiner mountain bike races.

Save My Baby (the Future King)!

The world's largest mountain bike race is the Birkebeiner. It attracts nearly 20,000 people to the Norwegian town of Lillehammer every August. The course is 57.2 miles (92.1 km), primarily over fire roads in the mountains surrounding the town. The race commemorates an incident during the Norwegian civil war era (1130–1240). Two Birkebeiners (people so poor that they wore shoes made of birch bark rather than leather) carried year-old Haakon Haakonsson, the heir to the throne, to safety on their cross-country skis. The toddler later became King Haakon IV and ended the civil wars. The original Birkebeiner was a cross-country ski race that began in 1932. The mountain bike version debuted in 1993. In both races, entrants must wear a backpack weighing at least 7.7 pounds (3.5 kg), which symbolizes young Haakon's weight during his long-ago flight.

Enjoying the Ride

Like other extreme sports, mountain biking serves as the impetus for several aspects of pop culture. These provide avenues of enjoyment when you're relaxing between rides.

Youth sports author Matt Christopher's 2005 book *The Extreme Team: Wild Ride* centers around Jonas, who joins a trail-clearing group in early spring. He gets in trouble when he rides on a closed course and blames someone else. Christopher also wrote *Mountain Bike Mania* (2007). When the main character, Will Matthews, discovers that he has a passion for mountain biking, the time he spends on the sport threatens his long-time friendship with Danny. The book also examines themes such as responsible use of public spaces and the need for bike riders to respect hikers who use the same trails as they do.

Another popular sports series for young readers comes from Jake Maddox. In *Mountain Bike Hero* (2011), Jonah and his younger brother Shawn bring their mountain bikes with them when they visit their grandfather. They're disappointed that their surroundings are almost totally flat, except for Crooked Hill—which their grandfather tells them is cursed. When Shawn disappears during a storm, Jonah must deal with the curse and find Shawn.

The author/illustrator team of Chris and Robin Lawrie has produced the Ridge Riders graphic novel series. It focuses on the mountain bike adventures of Slam Duncan and his friends. They enjoy their sports while remaining environmentally conscious. In *Paintball Panic* (2007), the group opposes a developer who wants to pack their favorite riding hill with new houses. They enter a paintball tournament the developer sponsors in order to win over the townspeople. When the tournament ends badly, the townspeople realize that they don't want the development. In *Cheat Challenge* (2007), Slam accidentally stumbles across the course map of a new race he and his friends are planning to enter. Slam wants to keep the information secret so that they don't cheat in order to win. But practicing on the wrong course puts them in danger.

For the incredible true story of Rebecca Rusch, check out her 2014 book *Rusch to Glory: Adventure, Risk, & Triumph on the Path Less Traveled*. It details her life story from her upbringing as a "normal" kid in Chicago who suffered from **bulimia** to becoming one of the biggest superstars in women's mountain biking.

Mountain biking has also inspired some video games that seek to reproduce the sport's excitement. One is *Downhill Domination* (2003). Players can choose from more than a dozen bikes and riders who perform stunts while zooming down steep mountainsides. *No Fear Downhill Mountain Bike Racing* (1999) also emphasizes downhill, with eight courses set on famously steep hills around the world. Players choose from among eight riders and customize their bike's tire pressure, suspensions, and gear ratios. *Mountain Bike Adrenaline* (2007) is more

OPPOSITE Experienced mountain bikers sometimes travel to China, where they traverse the mountains and valleys of the Gobi Desert, camping along the way.

cross-country-oriented, though a full range of tricks and stunts keeps players' interest at a high level.

A number of films help capture the allure of the sport. They look at some of the world's top riders in action, provide stunning scenery, and showcase the skills necessary for success. *Where the Trail Ends* (2012) follows five top-flight professional riders over a three-year period. They seek out some of the most spectacular, remote terrain to show off their abilities. Locales include the foothills of the Andes Mountains in Argentina, Nepal's sparsely populated Mustang Region, and China's Gobi Desert with its extremes of temperature. *Ride the Divide* (2010) chronicles the adventures of three entrants in what organizers term the world's most difficult mountain bike race. It stretches more than 2,700 miles (4,345 km) along the Great Divide of the Rocky Mountains from

OPPOSITE *Klunkerz* documents the early days of mountain bike racing, looking back to photos of the Repack races of the 1970s and featuring interviews with some of the people who started the sport.

Canada to Mexico. Conditions are primitive at best, and participants need to be very self-sufficient. Along the way, they climb more than 200,000 feet (60,960 m). That's like scaling Mt. Everest seven times!

And for a bit of history, take a look at *Klunkerz* (2006). It's a documentary examining the sport's origins in California. The film features lots of interviews with the biggest names in the Repack races as well as original footage and rare photographs from the era. It includes some spectacular wipeouts involving riders whose only protective equipment was long-sleeved shirts and jeans. *Klunkerz* received a number of positive critical reviews and has frequently been shown at film festivals.

Cyclical Trends

With mountain biking long since having passed the fad stage to become an important part of contemporary recreational and sports culture, numerous trends are likely to make it even more accessible and appealing. Finding places to ride will become easier as more trails open. The U.S. Geological Survey (USGS) has started including mountain bike trails on its state **topographic maps**. These maps are regularly updated. Many

OPPOSITE: Biking enthusiasts can take on treacherous terrain and enter mountain bike races all over the world, from Yak Attack high in the Himalayas to Ultra Raid de La Meije in the French Alps.

Cyclo-Cross

A close relative of mountain biking, cyclo-cross uses lightweight bikes with narrow, knobby tires and drop handlebars. Races consist of multiple laps on courses ranging between one and a half and two and a half miles (2.4–4 km). Surfaces include asphalt, grass, and hard-packed dirt and feature short, sharp climbs and numerous tight turns. Courses frequently include obstacles that require riders to dismount, carry their bikes over the obstacle, and then remount. The signature elements of the courses are stretches of mud that bikes can't cross. Riders dismount and carry their bikes through these stretches. Competitions usually race for a set amount of time, between 30 and 60 minutes. The object is to complete as many laps as possible during that time.

routes are provided to the USGS by the International Mountain Biking Association (IMBA), which in turn gets much of its information from individuals who upload maps and photos. "Finding, verifying, and consolidating data is expensive," says Brian Fox of USGS. "Partnering with non-government organizations that collect trails data through crowdsourcing is a great solution."

In addition, the Adventure Cycling Association (ACA) is compiling the U.S. Bicycle Route System (USBRS). In 2017, the system included more than 12,000 miles (19,312 km) of trails in 25 states and was poised to expand. "We will soon see this network reach every corner of America, from urban to rural areas," said ACA executive director Jim Sayer. "Given the project's momentum, we expect that, over time, the USBRS will become the largest official bicycle route network on the planet."

Bike technology is continually improving as well. For example, there has been a recent movement toward a single-ring chainring (with an 11-gear freewheel for maximum range) rather than the customary three. This gets rid of the front derailleur and therefore reduces weight and friction, simplifies shifting, and eliminates gear overlap. Because the single-ring isn't as simple as it sounds, it's still relatively pricey. As more work is done, affordability is likely to improve.

Electronic shifting has recently been introduced to mountain bikes. Manufacturers say that it will make shifting faster and more accurate. It may also allow simultaneous front and rear shifting via a pre-programmed system to provide the best possible gear combination.

More work is also being done on the structure of bikes themselves. For example, as its name suggests, the IziBi folding mountain bike can be folded in half and thereby fit in almost any vehicle. It's also easier to lock up since a chain can go easily through both wheels.

Mountain biking could get a boost if the Olympics

HUMNER
AMERICAN MONST
MONTEIRE MILITARY TECHNOLOGY
X HUMNER
HUMNER

OPPOSITE Several companies have developed bicycle models that fold. These designs might appeal to people with small vehicles and limited storage space, or those who must carry their bikes up several flights of stairs or onto buses or trains.

include downhill racing. Not surprisingly, downhill champion Gee Atherton favors its inclusion—but with a surprising twist. "I think downhill lends itself better to the spirit of the Winter Olympics," he explained. "If you look at how the Winter Games have changed, it would be a better fit." There's one major problem with this idea—under existing International Olympic Committee (IOC) rules, the only sports that can be in the Winter Olympics have to be contested on ice or snow.

Atherton does express the feelings of many people in the UCI, who would like as many cycling events in the Olympics as possible. While cross-country has been in the Olympics since 1996, UCI officials feel that the exposure of downhill—with its quick action—to so many viewers would increase its visibility and encourage people to take up the sport. "A huge part of downhill's appeal is its rawness," Atherton adds. "It's still got this wild feeling about it and it's not really like anything else."

Mountain biking is also gaining followers in endurance events. One of the earliest such events was Norway's Birkebeiner, first held in 1993. The following year came the Leadville (Colorado) Trail 100 MTB, which piggybacked onto the long-established Leadville Trail 100 footrace. Since then, more than 100 others have started up, both in the U.S. and overseas. Some, like Leadville, cover a definite distance, most commonly 100 miles (161 km). Others are based on time, usually from 3 to 24 hours.

A variation on these endurance events is a relay. Teams of four or more riders ride one at a time around the same course, for distances usually between 5 and 10 miles (8–16.1 km). When night falls, riders are responsible for providing their own lighting while teammates eat and sleep.

While most people credit the Repack racers in California with launching the mountain bike era, Crested Butte, Colorado, began its own program at about the same time. Fifteen riders set out on a trek that included a 13,000-foot (3,962 m) mountain pass. Only two managed to ride the entire distance, but two years later, Charlie Kelly and other Marin County riders joined them for another try. That began Fat Tire Bike Week (now called Crested Butte Bike Week), which not only continues to grow but also serves as a model for similar events elsewhere. Events include a 7-mile (11.3 km) downhill race in which entrants aren't allowed to pedal, a 40-mile (64.4 km) cross-country race over especially rugged terrain, a carnival, and more.

A more recent trend is riding indoors ... or even

OPPOSITE As the sport of mountain biking continues to grow and change, more bike parks and trails will be developed for riders of all skill levels to enjoy.

underground. Ray's Indoor Mountain Bike Park opened in 2004 in an abandoned parachute factory in Cleveland, Ohio. The site features more than 100,000 square feet (9,290 sq m) of space for all ability levels and incorporates obstacles such as loops, jumps, teeter-totters, suspension bridges, and stretches of logs.

In 2015, the Mega Underground Bike Park opened in an abandoned limestone mine in Louisville, Kentucky. It is likely the only underground bike park in the world and the largest indoor facility in the U.S. Its more than 320,000 square feet (29,729 sq m) include 45 trails with plenty of dirt mounds. The temperature is a steady 60 °F (15.6 °C). "This is the all-time best thing that has ever happened to cycling in Louisville," said local bicycle shopkeeper Derek Fetko. "When it's finished, this park is going to go a long way to help the Louisville mountain biking and BMX community become more competitive in the racing world."

Mountain biking has come a long way since its origins in the hills overlooking San Francisco Bay. While some people still love the thrill of going downhill as fast as possible, many more love the sport as a way of getting out into the woods or meadows and simply enjoying the silence and serenity of nature. For others, it's a healthy way to get around town. No matter what their reasons for riding, mountain bike riders have firmly cemented their sport's extreme status.

Glossary

adrenaline	a substance produced by the body, often when physically or emotionally stressed, characterized by increased blood flow and heightened excitement
bulimia	an eating disorder characterized by excessive eating, followed by vomiting and feelings of depression
coaster brake	a brake activated by pushing down on the pedals
components	parts of a larger whole, such as a machine
hydraulic	operated by a liquid moving under pressure in an enclosed space
pneumatic tires	tires made of reinforced rubber and filled with compressed air
sprockets	toothed wheels in which the teeth engage the links of a chain
topographic maps	maps showing detailed features of the land, such as mountains, hills, and creeks
tread	the part of a wheel making contact with the ground; bike treads have grooves and/or knobs for traction
wheelbase	the distance between the two wheels on a bike

Selected Bibliography

Berto, Frank J., Charles Kelly, and Rob van der Plas. *The Birth of Dirt: Origins of Mountain Biking*. 3rd ed. San Francisco: Cycle, 2015.

Forth, Clive. *The Mountain Bike Skills Manual: Fitness and Skills for Every Rider*. Guilford, Conn.: Falcon Guides, 2011.

Geall, Steve, and Robin Kitchin. *The Ultimate Guide to Mountain Biking*. New York: Lyons Press, 2001.

Hurst, Robert. *The Art of Mountain Biking: Singletrack Skills for All Riders*. Guilford, Conn.: Falcon Guides, 2012.

Lopes, Brian, and Lee McCormack. *Mastering Mountain Bike Skills.* 2nd ed. Champaign, Ill.: Human Kinetics, 2010.

McKnight, James. *Mountain Biking: Skills, Techniques, Training*. Ramsbury, Wiltshire, UK: Crowood Press, 2013.

Rusch, Rebecca. *Rusch to Glory: Adventure, Risk, & Triumph on the Path Less Traveled*. Boulder, Colo.: Velo Press, 2014.

Zinn, Lennard. *Zinn and the Art of Mountain Bike Maintenance*. 5th ed. Boulder, Colo.: Velo Press, 2010.

Websites

Adventure Cycling Association

https://www.adventurecycling.org/

This is the official website of the ACA, a nonprofit organization that encourages people to travel by bicycle. It includes route maps, a variety of organized tours, *Adventure Cyclist* magazine, and many additional resources.

International Mountain Bicycling Association

https://www.imba.com/

An organization that promotes mountain biking throughout the world, the IMBA emphasizes building new trails and maintaining existing ones. It also facilitates foreign tours, instructor training, bike-friendly laws, and more.

Note: Every effort has been made to ensure that any websites listed above were active at the time of publication. However, because of the nature of the Internet, it is impossible to guarantee that these sites will remain active indefinitely or that their contents will not be altered.

Index